P9-CZV-263

SAM'S *Pet* TEMPER

For my parents, Asish and Debi — S.B.

Kids Can Press acknowledges the financial support of the Government of Ontario, through the Ontario Media Development Corporation's Ontario Book Initiative; the Ontario Arts Council; the Canada Council for the Arts; and the Government of Canada, through the CBF, for our publishing activity.

Published in Canada by
Kids Can Press Ltd.
25 Dockside Drive
Toronto, ON M5A 0B5

Published in the U.S. by
Kids Can Press Ltd.
2250 Military Road
Tonawanda, NY 14150

www.kidscanpress.com

Kids Can Press is a Corus™ Entertainment company

The artwork in this book was rendered in mixed media (pencil, gouache and Photoshop).
The text is set in Adobe Caslon Pro.

Edited by Yvette Ghione and Yasemin Uçar
Designed by Karen Powers

This book is smyth sewn casebound.
Manufactured in Shenzhen, China, in 3/2014 by C & C Offset

CM 14 0 9 8 7 6 5 4 3 2 1

Library and Archives Canada Cataloguing in Publication

Bhadra, Sangeeta, author

Sam's pet temper / written by Sangeeta Bhadra ; illustrated by Marion Arbona.

ISBN 978-1-77138-025-6 (bound)

I. Arbona, Marion, 1982–, illustrator II. Title.

PS8603.H33S24 2014 jC813'.6 C2013-908218-2

SAM'S *Pet* TEMPER

WRITTEN BY *Sangeeta Bhadra* ILLUSTRATED BY *Marion Arbona*

KIDS CAN PRESS

Sam had a new pet. A pet of his very own. He found it at the playground that afternoon.

The playground was full of kids. Sliding, swinging, teetering, tottering. Wherever Sam went, he had to wait his turn.

Wait to slide. Wait to swing. Wait to teeter. Wait to totter.

Wait, wait, wait, wait, wait!

Sam was tired of waiting.
Waiting made him mad!
He got madder and madder
until he was the maddest he had
ever been in his whole life.

Suddenly, something jumped in among the kids. The thing ran around in circles, shoving and tripping and pinching and stomping.

Within seconds, the playground was empty except for Sam and the thing.

It was hanging upside down from the monkey bars, grinning at him.
Sam had never seen anything like it before, but he knew what it was.

It was a Temper.

The Temper had cleared off the playground just for Sam! No more waiting! Sam played to his heart's content all afternoon long. Sometimes other kids tried to join in, but the Temper just bared its teeth and growled fiercely.

When it was time to leave, Sam called out, "Hey, do you want to come home with me?" The Temper bounded into Sam's arms and licked him across the face.

The walk home was fascinating. The Temper was so funny! Sam knew they were going to be the best of friends.

When they arrived home, Sam ran to the backyard so he and his new pet could play in his tree house.

"Sorry, Sam," said Sam's mother. "It's almost suppertime."

On the way into the house, the Temper slammed the door.

"Sammy …" warned his mother.

The Temper kicked the wall.

“Sammy! What’s gotten into you?” asked his mother.

“It’s not me,” said Sam. “It’s my Temper.”

“Well, control your temper,” said his mother. “Now get washed up for supper.”

Sam told the Temper, “You have to be good at home, okay?”

The Temper purred.

During supper, the Temper hid under the table.

"Sam splashed up the bathroom," announced Sam's big sister.

The Temper gave her a kick in the shins.

"Ow! Sam kicked me!" she yelled.

"It wasn't me! It was my Temper!" Sam yelled back.

“That’s enough,” said Sam’s mother. “Sit still and eat your spaghetti or go to your room.”

The Temper picked up Sam’s plate and dumped it on the floor.

"Sam!" said Sam's mother. "I am nearing my limit!"

"But it wasn't me. It was my Temper. Here, I'll show you my Temper!" cried Sam.

"Upstairs, young man," said Sam's father. "The supper table is no place for tempers."

The Temper giggled and followed Sam upstairs.

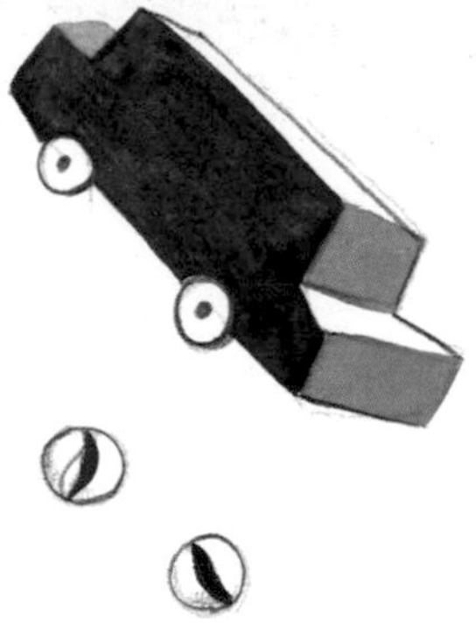

Having a Temper was more trouble than Sam had imagined.

"Go away!" he said. The Temper smiled sweetly, turned two cartwheels and bounced onto his bed. It tossed Sam's toys and pillows into the air and juggled them with its feet. Sam was starting to wish he didn't have a Temper.

In the morning,
the Temper wasn't there.
Sam checked under
the bed: no Temper.
He got dressed: no Temper.
He ate his breakfast:
no Temper.
"Phew!" said Sam.
He brushed his teeth and
skipped out the door …

Then he saw it, waiting at the curb.
Sam ignored it and kept walking.
The Temper followed,
whistling a little tune.

Sam usually liked school, but that morning was a disaster. The Temper scribbled over Rory's artwork, helped itself to Lucy's cookies and snapped all of the green crayons in half.

"You need a time-out," said Sam's teacher.

So Sam sat. And while he sat, the Temper did something truly terrible.

The principal called Sam's mother to pick him up from school early.

"You'll spend the rest of the afternoon in your room, thinking about what you've done, mister!" his mom said.

"But Mom, it wasn't my fault. It's my terrible Temper!"

"No more excuses, Samuel," said his mother. "Tempers cause trouble. That's what they do. Now *you* have to do something about *it*."

"I can't!" Sam cried.

"Sam, if you don't control your temper, no one can control it for you."

Sam was finally allowed to go to the playground on Saturday. His Temper tagged along. “Why won’t you leave me alone?” wailed Sam. The Temper pasted a juicy kiss on Sam’s nose and ran off to dig up a flower bed.

The playground was filling up quickly. Sam ran to the slide, but others beat him to it. With a yip and a growl, the Temper dashed over. As Sam watched it pounce, he began to feel a very different kind of mad.

“No!” Sam shouted.

The Temper blinked at him, then shuffled over to bite at a kid’s shoe.

“No!” said Sam as he clamped a hand over the Temper’s mouth.

The Temper reached out to grab another kid’s ponytail.

“No!” Sam grabbed the Temper’s arm.

The Temper struggled. What should Sam do?

Think, think, think …

Whenever his father was frazzled, he’d count to ten. Sam tried it.

One, two, three, four,

five, six, seven,

eight, nine,

ten.

The Temper squirmed.
The Temper kicked.
Sam thought harder.

Aha! His teacher got the class to settle down by saying their ABCs backward.

Sam tried it.

ZYXWVUTSRQP-P-P-

The Temper hissed.

It thrashed.

It lashed out like a giant, angry snake.

Sam gulped, and held on tight.

The Temper growled.

It snarled.

It roared like a ferocious lion.

Sam held on even tighter.

The Temper grumbled.
It rumbled.
It thundered like a furious storm cloud.

Sam said, "Terrible Temper, don't you know
that I'm stronger than you?"

He closed his eyes and took a deep breath … then he let it out s-l-o-w-l-y.

Something felt different. Sam opened one eye, then the other.

The Temper had stopped struggling. It was sitting at Sam's feet, frowning at him. Sam let out a laugh. He had done it! He had actually controlled his Temper.

Sam had a wonderful afternoon with the other kids. He called to the Temper to join them, but it preferred to sulk in a corner by itself.

All too soon, it was time to go home.
Sam whistled to his pet Temper. It didn't
come rushing over. It was staring at a screaming
toddler in a pink stroller. Sam started to walk away.
When he reached the edge of the park, he looked back.
The Temper tossed the little girl's shoes into the sandbox.
She shrieked with laughter. The Temper giggled.
Sam smiled and skipped home. If a Temper ever
found him again, he'd know what to do.